foreword by Joni Eareckson Tada

JUST LIKE
EVERYBODY
ELSE

by Jim Pierson

illustrated by Kathy Parks

STANDARD
PUBLISHING
Cincinnati, Ohio

To Norma, for thirty wonderful years

Editor: Diane Stortz
Designer: Coleen Davis

The Standard Publishing Company, Cincinnati, Ohio
A division of Standex International Corporation
© 1993 by The Standard Publishing Company
All rights reserved.
Printed in the United States of America
00 99 98 97 96 95 94 93   5 4 3 2 1

Library of Congress Catalog Card Number 93-16187
ISBN 0-87403-842-1
Cataloging-in-Publication data available

Joni Eareckson Tada is the founder and president of Joni and Friends, a Christian ministry to people with disabilities. Joni became a quadriplegic after a diving accident when she was seventeen. She is an internationally known mouth artist and the author of many best-selling books. Joni lives in Los Angeles with her husband, Ken.

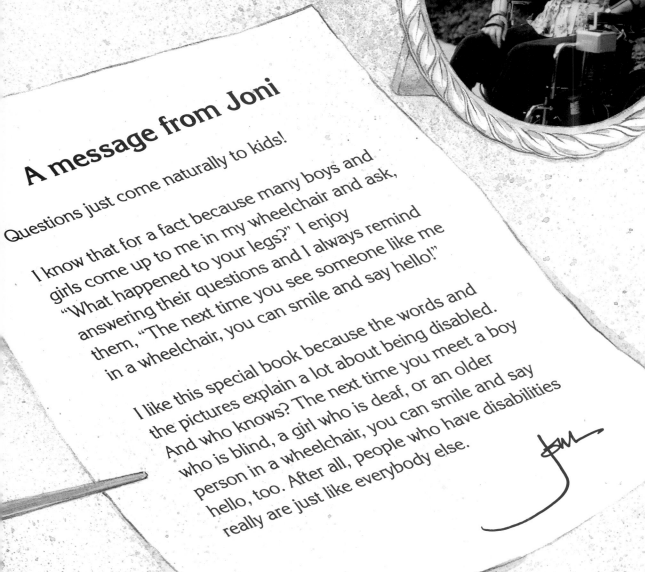

A message from Joni

Questions just come naturally to kids!

I know that for a fact because many boys and girls come up to me in my wheelchair and ask, "What happened to your legs?" I enjoy answering their questions and I always remind them, "The next time you see someone like me in a wheelchair, you can smile and say hello!"

I like this special book because the words and the pictures explain a lot about being disabled. And who knows? The next time you meet a boy who is blind, a girl who is deaf, or an older person in a wheelchair, you can smile and say hello, too. After all, people who have disabilities really are just like everybody else.

For the Adult Using This Book

This book is meant to be shared with a child or a group of children. Take time to discuss the story and its concepts. The explanations that you offer need not be long. Check page 32 of this book for sample answers to questions you may be asked.

As you read, notice how Granddaddy relates to persons with disabilities and how he relates to Derek. Both traits are essential for helping Derek learn to respond positively to Amy, the new girl in his class. You are a model for the children you teach or parent, so learn to demonstrate the same understanding and awareness that Granddaddy does. Having some basic information will help you:

- **Children often see disabling conditions as disease.** Offering reassurance that disabilities cannot be "caught" will usually be enough.

- **When children mimic the characteristics of people with disabilities, they likely are exploring how it would feel if they themselves were disabled.** Children can better grasp concepts they can act out. Do not scold for such behavior. Do explain that it is only appropriate to mimic when the child is alone, not when others are present, and never in front of anyone with a disability.

- **"Don't stare," the standard advice for years, can leave the wrong impression.** If told not to stare, the child receives a negative signal. Looking is a method of learning. Teach children the difference between a friendly look and an unkind stare.

- **Children often need help to see the person and not the diagnosis.** Help children realize that all people have feelings and sometimes struggle with them. Encourage children to talk with persons with disabilities. Begin by introducing them to an outgoing, positive adult. Remind children that they don't need to be afraid to touch the person with whom they are speaking.

- **Some traditionally accepted explanations are not really helpful to children.** For example, "We are all handicapped in some way" doesn't make sense to a child whose friend with cerebral palsy cannot run and jump like he does; the child knows that his only "handicap" is braces on his teeth! Also avoid "Persons with disabilities are special." The truth is that every person is special in God's sight (John 3:16).

- **Children can be encouraged to do something for people with disabilities.** A note, a card, a small gift, or a visit are normal ways of expressing concern. Such actions can lead to more involvement in the lives of persons with disabilities, who are, after all, just like everybody else.

—Jim Pierson
Knoxville, Tennessee
1993

On Friday afternoon, Derek's teacher, Miss Brown, made an announcement.

"We will have a new student on Monday," said Miss Brown. "Her name is Amy. She has cerebral palsy. Amy uses a wheelchair and crutches, but she enjoys learning just like all of you. Let's be friendly and help Amy feel comfortable here."

I don't know if I will like having Amy in my class, Derek thought. *I won't know what to say or do.*

The next morning, on the way to the zoo
with Granddaddy, Derek talked about Amy and
his scary feelings. Derek talked so much he was
surprised when he looked out the window —
they were already at the zoo!

There was a parking space near the entrance, but Granddaddy drove right by it.

"The sign says that space is reserved for people with disabilities," Granddaddy said. He found another place to park.

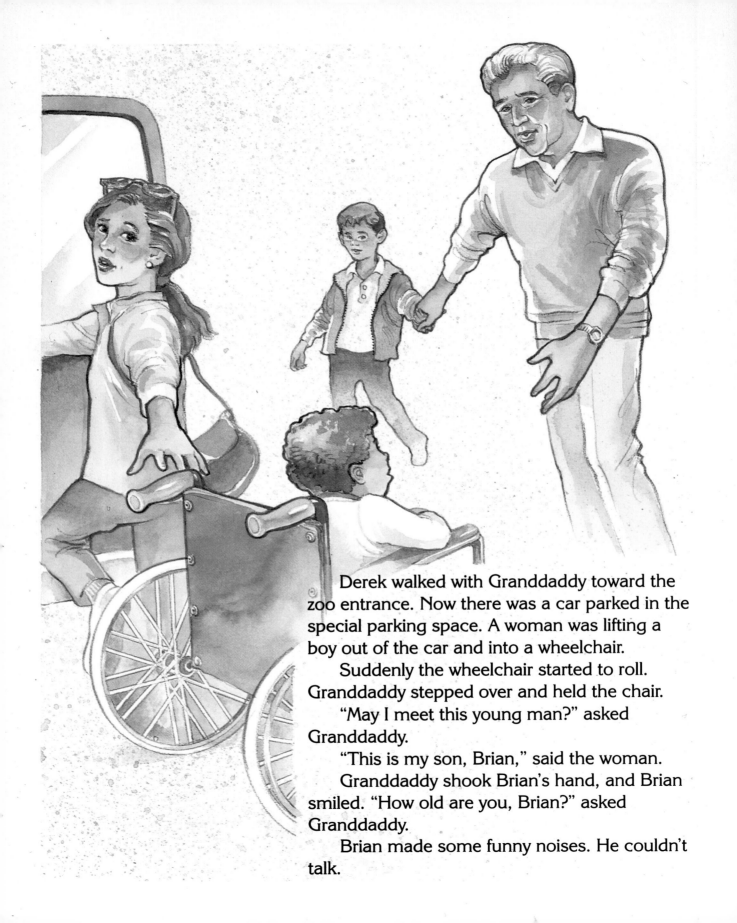

Derek walked with Granddaddy toward the zoo entrance. Now there was a car parked in the special parking space. A woman was lifting a boy out of the car and into a wheelchair.

Suddenly the wheelchair started to roll. Granddaddy stepped over and held the chair.

"May I meet this young man?" asked Granddaddy.

"This is my son, Brian," said the woman.

Granddaddy shook Brian's hand, and Brian smiled. "How old are you, Brian?" asked Granddaddy.

Brian made some funny noises. He couldn't talk.

Quickly Granddaddy said, "Are you six?"
Brian nodded his head yes.
"This is my grandson, Derek," said
Granddaddy. "He is also six."
Derek shook Brian's hand as Granddaddy
had done. Brian's hand felt just like his own.

Granddaddy asked Brian's mother what caused Brian's problem.

"CP — cerebral palsy," she replied. "His brain was damaged at birth. He won't ever be able to learn normally, walk, or talk."

Derek was listening carefully. When he and Granddaddy went to watch the elephants, Derek had a question.

"The new girl coming to my class has CP like Brian," he said. "But she can talk and learn. Why can't Brian talk and learn?"

"All CP is caused by damage to the brain," said Granddaddy. "Some people are born with it. Other people have been hurt in accidents. Some cerebral palsy is mild, like Amy's. Some, like Brian's, is worse."

"We shook hands with Brian," said Derek. "I'm afraid we will get CP."

"You can't catch CP," said Granddaddy. "It isn't a disease."

Derek felt a lot better.

The bird show was about to begin. Derek and Granddaddy were just in time to see it. They sat next to a mother and her daughter.

"Do you want to see the eagle get his lunch?" the announcer asked the audience. Everyone clapped and shouted, "Yes!"

"Please move to the center of your row so the eagle has a clear flight path," said the announcer.

Derek and Granddaddy and the mother moved, but the girl didn't.
Her mother tapped her on the shoulder and made signs with her hands.

Then the girl moved — and just in time!
The eagle swooped down from his perch
and got a fish from a pond in front of the stage.
Then he flew to a nearby tree to eat his lunch
while everyone cheered.

Next, Derek and Granddaddy went to see
the giraffes. "I'd hate to be a giraffe with a sore
throat!" joked Granddaddy.

The mother and daughter from the bird
show had come to watch the giraffes too.
Granddaddy smiled at them. "Hello," he said.
"Are you having fun at the zoo?"

Derek noticed that the girl was staring at
Granddaddy's lips. *And what is that thing
hanging on her ear?* he wondered.

When the girl said hello to Granddaddy, her voice sounded funny, and she didn't seem to want to talk.

The girl and her mother left, and Granddaddy and Derek stopped to get a drink. "That little girl has a hearing loss," Granddaddy explained. "Did you see her hearing aid? It helps make some sounds louder."

"Why didn't you just talk louder?" asked Derek.

"It doesn't help very much," said Granddaddy. "And it makes lip reading much harder."

"That girl's voice sounded funny," said Derek.

"That is how voices sound to her," said Granddaddy, "so that is the way she learned to talk."

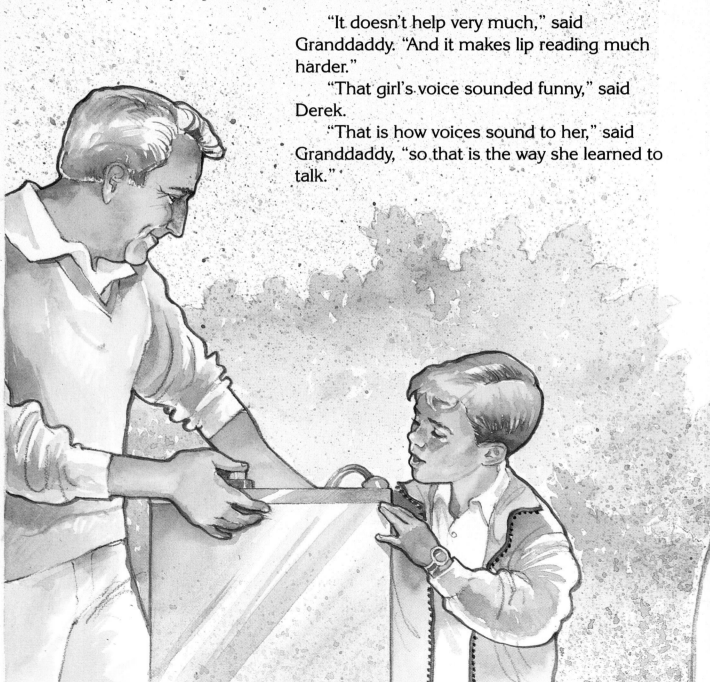

"She didn't want to talk very much," said Derek.

"People with disabilities are just like everybody else," Granddaddy said. "They don't all feel the same way about their problems. Some resent having a disability. Some think they are being treated like children. Some are fine."

Derek and Granddaddy had a great time at the zoo. They saw seals that swam so fast, and bears sleeping in the warm sun.

They watched monkeys swinging and chattering in their cages.

Then Derek and Granddaddy went to eat curly fries at Derek's favorite restaurant.

A man wearing dark glasses came into the restaurant with his dog.

Derek stopped eating and nudged Granddaddy.

"The dog is a guide dog," said Granddaddy. "He is trained to help his master, who is blind. Guide dogs are allowed in restaurants."

"Can I pet him?" asked Derek.

"Not while he is wearing his harness. That means he is working."

"Does the man need our help?" asked Derek.

"I don't think so," said Granddaddy. "He looks like he is doing just fine. But if you ever think a person with a disability does need your help, always ask him first. Treat someone with a handicap just like everybody else."

A family sat down at the next table. The boy in the family looked different somehow.

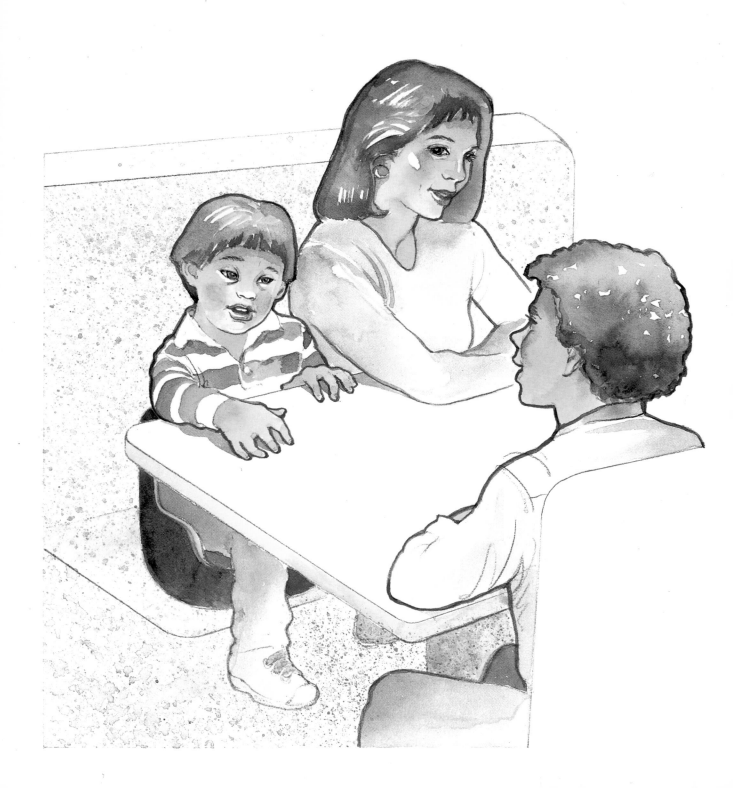

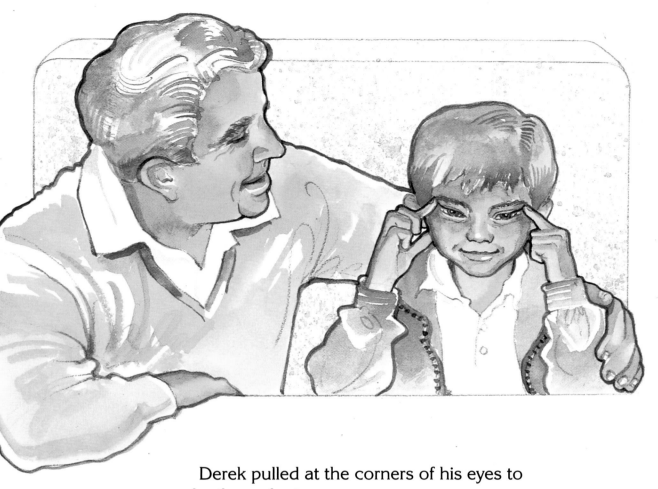

Derek pulled at the corners of his eyes to make them slant.

"What are you doing?" asked Granddaddy.

"I'm making my eyes look like that boy's," said Derek.

"Well," said Granddaddy, "the boy might think you are making fun of him. Other people might think so too. So whenever you want to pretend to have a disability, to see what it would be like, always do that when you are alone."

Derek ate a second helping of curly fries. "What is wrong with that boy, anyway?" he asked.

"He has Down syndrome," said Granddaddy. "People with Down syndrome have slanted eyes, short fingers, speech problems, and mental retardation. Mental retardation means not being able to learn as quickly as you and I do."

The server came to take the family's order. Derek heard her ask the mother what the boy wanted. The boy looked embarrassed.

Kids like to order by themselves, thought Derek.
He feels just like everybody else.

The boy's mother told the server to ask her son
what he wanted. He ordered curly fries!

Granddaddy needed to do some shopping.
So Derek and Granddaddy drove to the mall.
Outside the gift shop, Granddaddy saw a
friend and stopped to talk to him. Instead of a
right hand, the man had a hook. Derek's scary
feelings started to come back.

Oh, no! Was Granddaddy shaking hands with the hook?

"I want you to meet my grandson," said Granddaddy. "Derek, this is Mr. Henry." Granddaddy told Mr. Henry about the trip to the zoo, the curly-fry lunch, and the new girl in Derek's class.

"People with disabilities enjoy attention just like everybody else," Mr. Henry said to Derek. "We usually don't mind talking about our condition, especially with friends. Do you have any questions you would like to ask me?"

"What happened to your arm?" asked Derek.

"When I was a little boy, I was in a car accident," said Mr. Henry. "My hand and arm were badly injured and could not be fixed, so the doctors had to remove them. Now I have an artificial arm and this hook."

Derek and Granddaddy said good-bye to Mr. Henry and went into the gift shop. Derek felt good. His scary feelings were gone. He had learned so much today!

Derek thought it would be a good idea to buy a card for Amy. While Granddaddy did his shopping, Derek looked too. He found a card with a picture of a kitten on the front and paid for it himself.

Then Derek asked Granddaddy to help him write a note for Amy.

"That's a great idea!" said Granddaddy.

They found a table in the food court. Granddaddy printed Derek's message on a sheet of paper and Derek copied it inside the card.

Then Derek put the card in the envelope and wrote "Amy" on the outside.

"Are you all ready for Monday now?" asked Granddaddy.

"Yes, I am," said Derek.

On Monday morning all the kids in Derek's class were talking about Amy and wondering when she would arrive.

Just before the bell rang, Amy came into the room, walking with her crutches. Her mother was pushing her wheelchair.

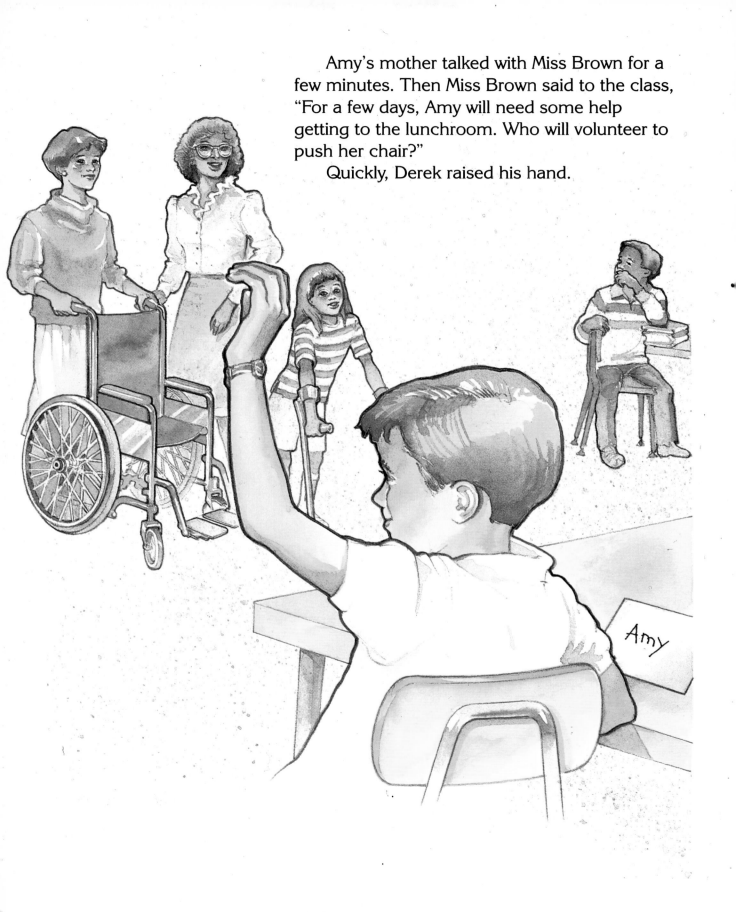

Amy's mother talked with Miss Brown for a few minutes. Then Miss Brown said to the class, "For a few days, Amy will need some help getting to the lunchroom. Who will volunteer to push her chair?"

Quickly, Derek raised his hand.

At lunchtime, when Miss Brown told Derek it was time to help Amy, he took the card from his book bag and handed it to Amy. She opened it as Derek pushed her down the hall.

Derek's card said,

Dear Amy,
 I'm glad you are
in our class.
 I want to be
your friend.
 I know that
you are just like
everybody else.
            Derek

Answers to Questions Children Ask

"What does the sign with a stick man sitting in a wheelchair mean?"

The stick man sitting in a wheelchair is a symbol for "handicap." This symbol has the same meaning all around the world. On a sign, the symbol is a way of asking all of us to be kind to people with disabilities. If the sign is over a parking place, it means that a person with a disability or someone driving for a person with a disability can park there. When you see the sign on a rest-room door, it means that the doors and stalls in the rest room are wider and the sinks are lower. Those things help a person in a wheelchair get in and out more easily.

"Why do some people get handicaps?"

We do not know the reason that some people have birth defects, accidents, or illnesses that cause them to have disabilities. We might know how the disability was caused but we may never know *why*. But every person is important and special, and everybody has a purpose for being alive (Philippians 1:6). We need to accept each person's strong points and weak points and enjoy one another's unique personalities.

"How should we talk about what is wrong with a person?"

Handicapped is not the best word; *disabled* is a better word. Say exactly what you mean. For example, say "persons with mental retardation" instead of "the mentally retarded" and "uses a wheelchair" instead of "wheelchair bound." Be positive, and always make the person more important than what is wrong with him or her.

"What makes someone have Down syndrome?"

Most people have 46 *chromosomes* in the cells of their body. We get 23 from our mother and 23 from our father. For some reason, some people have an extra chromosome. That 47th one makes the person have Down syndrome. It is a major cause of mental retardation.

"Why do some people talk with their hands?"

They actually talk with their hands *and* their eyes. People who are deaf learn to watch your lips when you talk. They also learn to make signs with their hands in order to express their thoughts. You may hear the words *lip reading, speech reading, signing,* and *finger spelling*. These are all ways that people who are deaf "talk." If you do not know sign language and you are going to be with a friend who is deaf, take some paper and a pencil and write what you want to say.

"How does an artificial arm or leg stay on?"

Most are held in place with straps and Velcro®. First the artificial arm or leg is fitted to the body of the person who needs it. Then the person is shown how to use the arm or leg. You might want to ask a person who uses an artificial arm or leg to tell you how it works. You will get a good answer.